Huckleberry Hash

OTHER YEARLING BOOKS YOU WILL ENJOY

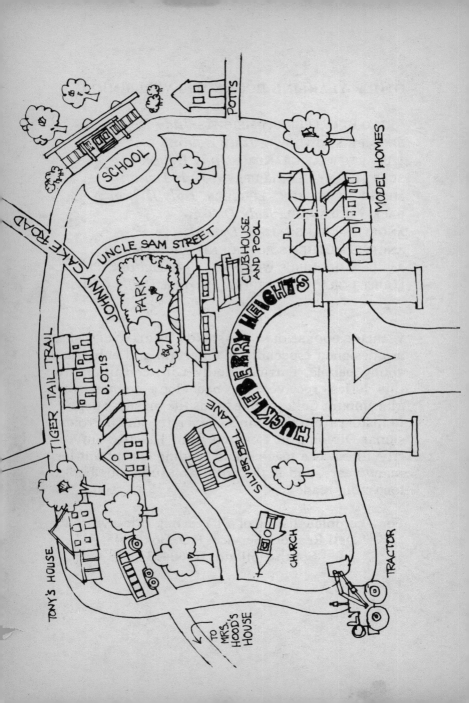

Huckleberry Hash

Judy Delton

Illustrated by Alan Tiegreen

A YEARLING BOOK

Published by
Dell Publishing
a division of
Bantam Doubleday Dell Publishing Group, Inc.
666 Fifth Avenue
New York, New York 10103

ISBN: 0-440-40325-1

Printed in the United States of America

September 1990

10 9 8 7 6 5 4 3 2 1

CWO

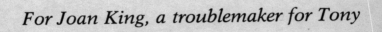

For Joan King, a troublemaker for Tony

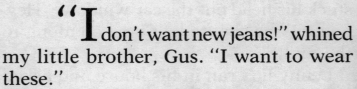

"**I** don't want new jeans!" whined my little brother, Gus. "I want to wear these."

We were all ready to go to Yankee Doodle Mall to get school clothes, and Gus wouldn't get in the car.

"My mom says I can wear these," said Punkin Head Maloney, Gus's friend. · Well, my friend too. "She lets me wear what I want to school."

Punkin Head had on some too-tight shorts. His T-shirt was tight too. And his bare stomach showed in between where his shirt and pants didn't meet. He was eating a big sweet roll.

My mom looked at Punkin Head.

"Maybe you should come with us, dear," she said.

"Let's get going," said my sister, Marcy. She's twelve. Gus is eight. And I'm ten. My name is Tony. Our last name is Doyle. We live with our mom in a new condo.

Punkin Head and Gus got in the car. My mom drove a little way and Gus stuck his head out the car window. "Hey, Lenny!" he shouted. "Come on along to the mall!"

Lenny Fox ran in his house and asked his mother if he could go. Then he dashed out and got in the car.

Marcy slid over in the backseat. "Pretty soon we'll have all of Huckleberry Heights in our car," she said.

"Hey, Edgar, want to come to the mall?" yelled Gus.

"Edgar's my friend," I said.

Edgar Allan Potts got in the front seat next to Gus.

"Let's get out of here!" yelled Marcy.

Just then my old girl friend Lily Camp came out of her house, and Marcy

yelled, "Hey, Lily! Want to come to the mall?"

"We have a pretty big load," said my mom.

"You said it," I said. Lily thought she was my girl friend. She hung on me and talked about mushy stuff. She even kissed me on the playground last year. I liked her all right, but I didn't want anyone to know it.

Lily jumped in the car, right onto my lap.

"We'll have to double up," said my mom, laughing. "Sit on laps. It isn't far."

Lily's hair was in my face. It smelled clean, like our towels when they come out of the wash. "What kind of shampoo do you use, anyway?" I said.

"Spring Bouquet," she said.

"I'm going to meet Aunt Fluffy for coffee," said my mom when we got there and Lily jumped out. Her curls bounced like little springs.

"You look around and meet me back

4

here in front of Dayton's at exactly one o'clock. Then we'll get school clothes."

I had the feeling my mom's idea of school clothes was not mine. She had us fixed in her mind at about four years old in striped T-shirts and those matching pants.

Last spring she got tired of our apartment in St. Paul and moved us all to a condo out here in the suburbs so we'd have fresh air and a barbecue in the backyard. At first there were no trees and the streets were all mud and we didn't have grass. We do now. We even have this big clubhouse with a swimming pool, and our new school opens this fall. It's like our own little town here in Huckleberry Heights. We have a dog too. His name is Smiley and he's a sheepdog. He'd be too big for our old apartment in St. Paul. But out here he has a nice yard and a doghouse.

Marcy ran off to some store where they do makeup make-overs, and Lily came with us to the pet store, where Lenny and I priced artificial bones that gave dogs good breath. I bought a big one for Smiley.

Then we went to the hobby shop and watched the model trains go around on a track. Through little tunnels and between little trees.

Out in the mall, Punkin Head bought a bag of popcorn and a candy bar. We sat on a bench by a dribbling water fountain and watched people walk by.

It was almost time to meet my mom when I noticed Gus wasn't with us. "Where's Gus?" I said.

Edgar and Lenny and Punkin Head and Lily looked around. "He's not here," said Punkin Head.

"I know that much," I snapped. "My mom wants to get him clothes, we better find him before one o'clock."

We ran up and down the mall looking. Lily kept stopping to look in store windows, but the rest of us checked everything. I ran back to the pet store to see if Gus was still hanging around the parrot that talked. He wasn't. I ran to the hobby store, and the food stands and the petting zoo. No Gus.

"He's too old to get kidnapped," said Lenny.

Kidnapped. I hadn't thought of that.

"And he can't get lost," said Edgar.

"He is lost," I said.

"He knows his way around here," said Edgar, shaking his head.

"He's just—" began Lenny. Just what? It was hard to finish that sentence. Gus didn't like to shop. The pet and hobby stores were the only places that would interest him.

We ran into Marcy with gook all over her face. She looked at her watch. "There is a place to report lost kids," she said. "A mall office or something."

I pictured us reporting Gus. "Last seen where?" the officer would mutter. I saw pictures of Gus flashing on TV screens on the six o'clock news. Cameras outside our house. HUCKLEBERRY HEIGHTS YOUTH DISAPPEARS, it would say in the morning paper. When my mom read that at breakfast, she'd be sure to know Gus was gone.

"Tony!" said Marcy, stamping her foot. "I asked you what he was wearing."

When last seen what was the victim wearing? They always asked that question.

Marcy was heading for the office without me. We were just passing the rest rooms when I heard this muffled voice. "Lemme out of here!" it said. "Help!"

"Listen," said Lily.

"It's Gus," Marcy said. We tried the door of the rest room. It wouldn't open.

"I can't get out of here!" screamed Gus.

"Turn the knob," said Marcy.

"I am. It won't open."

I gave the door a big kick. Nothing happened. It was a door made out of iron or something. No human being could rob those bathrooms. And who would want to steal a toilet anyway? It struck me as a dumb place to have a burglar-proof door.

"Be patient, Gus, we'll get you out," yelled Edgar, who had joined us.

Marcy went into the mall office, and before long some guys with screwdrivers and hammers and a crowbar took the door off its hinges and got Gus out.

"I thought I'd have to live in there," said Gus in relief.

"It's a good thing we heard you, or you'd be on the six o'clock news," I said.

"Maybe it's too late to get school clothes," said Punkin Head.

We dashed to Dayton's, where we were supposed to meet my mom.

"She's not even here," said Marcy.

We sat down on a mall bench to wait. In about ten minutes my mom and Aunt Fluffy came running up, all out of breath.

"Sorry we're late," said my mom. "But we found this fantastic sale. We got your school clothes without you. Things were going like hotcakes from the sale table. We didn't have time to come and get you to try them on."

"But I think we made some great

choices," said Aunt Fluffy. She held up a pair of pants that would fit a giant.

"They're roomy enough for you to wear next year too!" she said to me.

I began to hate Gus for going to the bathroom. If we'd been on time, maybe we could have stopped my mom from finding the sale table. It isn't that we're poor or anything. My mom owns her own faucet company, Trixie's Taps. Sales are just her hobby.

"Just feel this material," my mom was saying to Marcy. Marcy touched the T-shirt. It said I LOVE GRANDMA on the front of it.

"No one wears sale stuff," Marcy was whining. "It's all the stuff they couldn't sell because it's out-of-date. No one will buy it."

But Marcy was wrong. People did buy it. The next morning three kids on our block were wearing my corduroy pants.

My mom isn't unreasonable.
When Marcy cried about the T-shirt and
I explained how embarrassed Gus and I
would be to wear clothes we hated, she
said, "We will put them in the fire box
and buy you new ones."

My mom's fire box is in Marcy's closet.
It's filled with clothes we have (1) out-
grown or (2) hate.

"These clothes are perfectly good," my
mom said. "In case of a fire we'll be
glad we have them."

I never figured out why our good
clothes would burn up and these would
be untouched. But my mom said, "Silly,
I mean a fire somewhere else. A family

13

with lots of children. On the news they say, 'If any of you want to donate clothes to the fire victims, here is the number to call.' " The number was written down next to the TV guide.

We used these clothes for dress-up, too, like on Halloween. I was glad to donate the sale clothes to a good cause. We got new ones (that we picked out ourselves) on Saturday.

On Monday our new school opened. It seemed funny not to get on a school bus and ride for miles. I could get up ten minutes before school started now, eat breakfast, and walk real slow and still be there on time. Huckleberry Heights School was where this big empty lot used to be. Before the basement went in, we used to sit in the bottom of the pit. Right where the lunch room is now.

To get there I just walk right down Tiger Tail Trail, past the Otises' house (where Marcy's friend Daisy lives), cross Johnny Cake Road, and there I am. Edgar lives a little farther down on Uncle Sam Street, kind of near the clubhouse.

He can see the school from his bedroom window. That's a little too close for me. I don't like to think of school every time I look out my window.

Lenny and Edgar came by with new lunch boxes. Punkin Head came by with stiff new jeans on. "I can hardly bend," he said. His hair was wet and you could see the comb marks in it.

Marcy and Daisy Otis were hanging around in front of the new kid's house. His name was George Nelson. Marcy spent a lot of time in front of the mirror trying to look good to attract him. She and Daisy called it "luring" boys. When George came out, the girls looked surprised to see him.

"Why! Hey, there!" said Daisy. "Are you going to school too?"

What else would he be doing? He was thirteen and had a bunch of notebooks in his hand. He sure wasn't going off to war.

On the way to school, Lily caught up with us.

"Here," she said, taking a cupcake

out of her lunch box and handing it to me. "My mom made going-back-to-school cupcakes."

The cupcake had a little pencil on it, made out of frosting.

"This is a historic day," Lily said to me.

"What's historic about it?" said Punkin Head.

"Did the stock market drop?" asked Lenny. Lenny and his dad watched the stock market. Lenny was a real businessman.

"Did a space ship take off?" asked Edgar.

"It's more historic than that," said Lily. "My dad said this is the very first day our new school opens its doors. They put the date right in cement on the front of the building. And there's this time capsule they put in the wall so that in a thousand years someone will open it and find out how we lived now."

"Pooh," said Gus. "That's not historic. Schools open all the time."

When we got there, we found out Lily

was right. There was a cement block that said *This school first opened its doors on* . . . and then there was the date. And the new principal was standing on the brand-new front steps in a brand-new suit, saying, "Welcome to Huckleberry Heights School. Today is a momentous day. It is the first of many, many days in your new school, in your quest for knowledge."

He made it sound like a long haul. *Many, many days* sounded like we'd be here forever.

Inside it smelled like paint and chalk and soap and a little bit like something cooking on the stove.

"Look at these water fountains!" said Punkin Head with a whistle. He ran up to one. It didn't look like a fountain to me. There was this great big round pipe thing, and when you pressed it water came out. Ten kids could stand around it in a circle and all take a drink at once.

"My dad said these things are real

modern, no more long lines at drinking fountains," said Lenny.

It reminded me of a lot of horses around a watering hole in an old western movie.

Edgar and I and Lily found fifth grade, and Lenny and Punkin Head and Gus found third. Punkin Head should really have been in fourth, but he flunked kindergarten, so he was with Gus and Lenny.

"See you guys," I called. We waved to Marcy and Daisy and George. They were going down the hall where the older kids were.

Our new teacher was standing in our new classroom. She was not old and not young and not tall and not short. Everything looked kind of medium about her. She even had a medium voice.

"Just sit where you like today," she said, implying that by tomorrow she'd give us seats we didn't like. The desks were in a circle instead of in rows. This was a modern school. Lenny was right.

And the blackboards were green instead of black.

The teacher told us her name was Miss Roscoe. Then she gave a little talk about how lucky we were to have a brand-new school and be the first students on the first day blah blah blah and how historic a moment this stuff all was.

"There are a lot of things that are still unfinished," the teacher warned. I looked at the little piles of sawdust in the corners. And some bookshelves that weren't painted yet.

"There are a lot of bugs to be worked out in a new place," she went on. "But Rome wasn't built in a day, and we have to work things out as we go, don't we?" She smiled at us. Some of the kids nodded.

Just when she'd said that, bells started to ring.

"School's out already!" said Edgar, piling up his notebooks to leave.

"It's lunchtime," said Lily, getting out

her lunch box with the first-day-of-school cupcakes in it.

"It's recess," I said. "School can't be out already."

Miss Roscoe picked up the phone on her desk. "Hello, hello?" she said into it. Then she hung it up.

Some of the kids thought it was a fire drill and lined up real quick with their arms folded, the way we learned in the other school. They marched out the door onto the playground before anyone could stop them.

The bells kept ringing no matter what we did. Then a buzzing noise began. There was a lot of static, and we could hear a voice say, "Testing, one two, testing, one two three."

"This is your principal, Mr. Cummings," it finally said after a burst of banging and crashing. "As you know, there are a lot of bugs to work out in a new sys—" But then his voice faded and a sharp whistling noise began. Miss Roscoe was motioning us to sit down at our desks and relax. "The bells don't mean anything," she shouted over the din. "It will take a while before things all mesh."

Lily began eating her lunch.

Finally the whistlings and ringings stopped. Workers came in the room and began to adjust some wires. The kids on the playground came in. The clock on the wall said six o'clock. My watch said nine-thirty. I trusted my watch.

"I think we can begin our school day now," said Miss Roscoe, smiling. She passed out math books and geography books and spellers. She gave us name tags to help us get acquainted. And she asked for volunteers to tell about their summer.

Edgar waved his hand to tell about a film festival his father had taken the family to. Another kid named Ronnie told about going to day camp. I raised my hand to tell about Smiley's new doghouse.

"Yes, Anthony," said Miss Roscoe.

When I began to talk, some loud hammering began outside our door and no

one could hear me. Miss Roscoe closed the door, and I began again. The kids liked my story, and they clapped real loud. Just as I sat down in my desk a piece of loose plaster from the ceiling fell on my head. A cloud of plaster dust hung over me and made me sneeze. Edgar and Lily began to laugh.

Miss Roscoe dusted me off and asked if I was all right, and looked to see if there was a dent in my head. There wasn't. Then she called the custodian, who checked the ceiling and said it was safe.

"I think we all need a little recess," Miss Roscoe said, laughing. "Even if the recess bell has not rung."

At recess Gus stepped in wet cement, and the toilets didn't flush in the bathroom. In the afternoon we traced maple leaves onto yellow paper and cut them out to decorate the windows. I got an A on a spelling refresher quiz.

When we got home, we all had plaster dust in our hair.

"How was your first day in the new school?" asked my mom.